KU-343-072

READING CORNER

A Bunch of
Balloons

Written by
Anne Cassidy

Illustrated by
Philippe Dupasquier

W

FRANKLIN WATTS
LONDON•SYDNEY

Anne Cassidy

"I love shiny balloons. I always buy as many as I can for my parties – just like the boy in my story!"

Philippe Dupasquier

"This book was fun to illustrate. I wonder how many balloons it would take to get me off the ground?"

It was the day of Joe's party.

Mum bought ten balloons.

"Hold these," she told Joe.

7

Joe held on tight, but there were just too many balloons.

Joe had to let four balloons go.

The wind blew and blew.

13

The wind tugged and tugged.
A balloon floated away.

15

A dog barked and Joe jumped.

Another balloon floated away.

"Hurry up, Joe!" said Mum.

"I'm coming!" said Joe.

But he left a balloon behind.

A bird pecked and a balloon
went **BANG!**

A baby cried and cried.

"Have this balloon!" said Joe.

Joe had only one balloon left.

But a fat cat was sitting on the fence and he popped it!

POP

"Oh no! Where are all the balloons?" cried Joe's mum.

29

"No problem," said Joe's dad.
"I bought some balloons, too!"